THE CURSE OF THE Creepy Crypt

by Michael Anthony Steele
illustrated by Dario Brizuela

Batman created by Bob Kane with Bill Finger

STONE ARCH BOOKS
a capstone imprint

Published by Stone Arch Books,
an imprint of Capstone.
1710 Roe Crest Drive
North Mankato, Minnesota 56003
capstonepub.com

Library of Congress Cataloging-in-Publication Data
Names: Steele, Michael Anthony, author. | Brizuela, Dario, illustrator. |
Steele, Michael Anthony. Batman and Scooby-Doo! mysteries.
Title: The curse of the creepy crypt / by Michael Anthony Steele ;
illustrated by Dario Brizuela.
Description: North Mankato : Stone Arch Books, 2022. | Series: Batman and
Scooby-Doo! mysteries | Audience: Ages 8–11. | Audience: Grades 4–6. |
Summary: When an ancient Greek crypt at the Gotham City Museum of Natural
History is opened unleashing mythological monsters, the Mystery Inc. gang
team up with Batman and Batwoman to battle the creatures and uncover the
super-criminal behind the mayhem.
Identifiers: LCCN 2021054224 (print) | LCCN 2021054225 (ebook) |
ISBN 9781666335057 (hardcover) | ISBN 9781666335064 (paperback) |
ISBN 9781666335088 (pdf)
Subjects: LCSH: Scooby-Doo (Fictitious character)—Juvenile fiction. | Batman
(Fictitious character)—Juvenile fiction. | Superheroes—Juvenile fiction.
| Supervillains—Juvenile fiction. | Animals, Mythical—Juvenile fiction. |
Monsters—Juvenile fiction. | CYAC: Superheroes—Fiction. | Supervillains—
Fiction. | Animals, Mythical—Fiction. | Monsters—Fiction. | Mystery and
detective stories. | LCGFT: Detective and mystery fiction.
Classification: LCC PZ7.S8147 Cu 2022 (print) | LCC PZ7.S8147 (ebook) |
DDC [Fic]—dc23
LC record available at https://lccn.loc.gov/2021054224
LC ebook record available at https://lccn.loc.gov/2021054225

Designer: Tracy Davies

Printed and bound in the USA. 4882

TABLE OF CONTENTS

MEET BATMAN AND

BATMAN

While still a boy, Bruce Wayne watched his parents die at the hands of a petty criminal. After that tragic day, the young billionaire vowed to rid Gotham City of evil and keep its people safe. To achieve this goal, he trained his mind and body to become the World's Greatest Detective. Donning a costume inspired by a fearful run-in with bats at a young age, the Dark Knight now aims to strike the same sense of fear in his foes. But the Caped Crusader doesn't always work alone. He often teams up with other crime fighters, including Robin, Batgirl, Batwing, Batwoman, and even . . . Mystery Inc.

THE MYSTERY INC. GANG

Traveling in a van named the Mystery Machine, these meddling kids, and their crime-fighting canine, solve mysteries all over the country—even in Gotham City!

THE MYSTERY INC. GANG

Scooby-Doo

A happy hound with a super snout, Scooby-Doo is the mascot of Mystery Inc. He'll do anything for a Scooby Snack!

Shaggy Rogers

Shaggy is a laid-back dude who would rather search for food than clues . . . but he usually finds both!

Fred Jones, Jr.

Fred is the oldest member of the group. Friendly and fun-loving, he's a good sport—and good at them too.

Velma Dinkley

Velma is clever and book smart. She may be the youngest member of the team, but she's an old pro at cracking cases.

Daphne Blake

Brainy and bold, the fashion-forward Daphne solves mysteries with street smarts and a sense of style.

CHAPTER 1

THE GRAND OPENING

Velma adjusted her glasses as she leaned closer to the giant stone object. "The detail in these carvings is amazing," she said. "I see a griffin, a Cyclops, a minotaur . . . all kinds of Greek monsters."

"Like, mythical monsters, right?" Shaggy asked as he gazed at the crypt. "As in *not* real?"

Daphne patted him on the shoulder. "Don't worry, Shaggy. Those creatures are from ancient Greek myths. They're not real at all."

"That's right," Fred agreed.

Scooby-Doo breathed a sigh of relief. "Phew!"

The Mystery Inc. gang joined several other guests inside the Gotham City Museum of Natural History. Everyone was there to see the museum's newest exhibit, a large, sealed crypt from ancient Greece. While they waited for the big opening, servers milled through the crowd offering trays of food and drinks.

Fred pointed to more of the carvings. "Ooh, look. There's Cerberus, the three-headed dog."

"Ree heads?" Scooby asked.

Shaggy snickered as he grabbed a handful of snacks from a passing tray. "Yeah, Scoob! Like, more mouths to eat *more* tasty treats." He tossed three cheese-covered crackers toward his pal. Scooby-Doo downed all three in one bite.

"One routh works fine for me," Scooby said. He giggled and licked his lips.

"Cerberus was the ferocious beast that guarded the gates of the Underworld," Velma explained.

"You certainly know your Greek mythology," said a woman with glasses and a hijab. She smiled at the group. "I'm Dr. Deanna Coats."

"Wow! You're the archaeologist who found the crypt," Velma said. She shook the woman's hand. "It's an honor to meet you." Velma introduced herself and the rest of the gang.

Dr. Coats pointed up at the crypt. "I'm just happy to be able to share this with the world."

Shaggy snatched some more tidbits from another passing tray. "Like, I'm happy you're sharing so many snacks."

"Reah!" Scooby agreed.

Dr. Coats laughed. "Well, for that, you can thank my sponsor." She waved a man over. He was tall and wore a sharply pressed suit.

"Bruce Wayne," Daphne said.

"Hi, everyone," Bruce greeted. "It's good to see you again."

"Oh, good," Dr. Coats said. "You already know each other."

"Yes, but they may not know my cousin," Bruce said. He turned and nodded at an approaching woman with short red hair. "This is Kate Kane."

"Hello," Kate greeted. "Bruce was kind enough to invite me along." She glanced up at the crypt. "I have a special interest in mythological creatures."

"Like, as long as those monsters stay on the crypt, where they belong," Shaggy said.

Dr. Coats grinned. "I'm more interested in what's *inside* the crypt." She checked her watch. "And I think it's just about time for its grand opening!"

Bruce, Kate, and the Mystery Inc. gang joined the other guests as Dr. Coats turned to address the crowd.

"May I have your attention, please?" she asked. When the audience settled down, she continued, "I want to thank you all for coming, and I want to thank Bruce Wayne for making all of this possible."

The audience applauded, and Bruce Wayne smiled and nodded.

"Now, this Greek crypt has been sealed, airtight, for thousands of years," Dr. Coats continued. "There's no telling what kind of priceless treasures will be inside. Let's find out, shall we?"

One of the attendants brought her a crowbar, and she moved closer to the crypt. She raised the tool toward the edge of the sealed door but then stopped.

Dr. Coats pointed to a line of ancient writing carved into the stone. "I think I should mention that this says that a deadly curse will be put on anyone who opens this."

Scooby-Doo's ears shot up. "A rurse?"

"Like, no one said anything about a curse," Shaggy whispered.

Velma shook her head. "Oh, Shaggy. You know there's no such thing as curses."

Shaggy gulped. He wasn't so sure.

"But don't worry," Dr. Coats said with a chuckle. "Since I'm the one opening it, everyone else should be safe."

The audience laughed as the archaeologist moved back toward the crypt. She slid the end of the crowbar into a thin gap and grunted as she pried open the door.

WHOOOOOOSH!

Dusty air rushed out of the crypt as the door slowly swung open. Everyone backed away and coughed as the dust cloud grew larger. It was so thick that it hid Dr. Coats, the crypt, everything.

Ki-KLANG!

A metallic noise echoed in the hall.

When the dust thinned out, Fred pointed at the crypt. "Where's Dr. Coats?" he cried.

The archaeologist was gone. The crowbar lay on the ground where she had stood.

Suddenly, the lights flickered, and a deep growl echoed throughout the museum.

GRRRRRRRRRR!

"Ruh-Roh!" Scooby-Doo said as he jumped into Shaggy's arms.

Shaggy's knees knocked together as he shook with fright. "Like, what were you saying about curses?"

Velma scratched her head and glanced around. "I'm sure there's a logical explanation for all this."

"There is," Daphne said as she pointed to one of the corridors. "Look!"

A giant beast lumbered down the large hallway. It had the body of a lion and the head and wings of an eagle.

"A griffin," Velma said. "But they're not supposed to be real."

"It looks pretty real to me," Shaggy said.

The beast glared at the crowd and opened its large, beaked mouth. *ROOOOOOAR!*

The audience screamed with terror.

Bruce turned to his cousin. "Let's get these people out of here!"

The crowd didn't need much help. They were already running toward the main exit.

Bruce Wayne and Kate Kane chased after them, but not to escape—they had other plans in mind. No one else knew that they secretly fought crime as Batman and Batwoman.

As everyone else fled the museum, the Mystery Inc. gang hid behind the crypt. Daphne was shocked to see Shaggy and Scooby chowing down on food from one of the serving trays.

"How can you eat at a time like this?" Daphne asked.

"Like, there's about to be a bunch of running, screaming, mystery solving, and monster trapping . . . ," Shaggy replied. "We're going to need our strength."

"Reah," Scooby-Doo agreed. "What he said."

The giant beast lumbered closer to their hiding place.

"Okay, gang," Fred said. "We need a plan to take this monster down."

"Or maybe we don't," Velma replied, pointing above them. "Look!"

A dark figure swooped in from above—it was Batman! As the Dark Knight glided closer, he threw three special Batarangs at the creature.

BAM! BAM! BAM! The weapons exploded as they struck the beast.

The gang peeked out from behind the crypt as Batman lightly touched down in front of the creature. Smoke completely hid the griffin, but the haze quickly cleared as it flapped its huge wings and rose off the ground.

"Jinkies!" Velma said. "That thing is tougher than it looks."

Batman stood ready for battle as the griffin dove for him. It spread its claws, ready to attack.

POP-WRRRR! A grapnel shot into view and wrapped around the griffin's neck. Another caped figure was at the other end of the line.

"It's Batwoman!" Daphne shouted.

The crime fighter's boots slid across the floor
as she tried to hold tight against the struggling
creature. Batman rushed to her aid and grabbed
the line. The two fought to hold on as the beast
rose higher and higher.

"Come on," Fred said. "Let's help!"

Fred led the way as the Mystery Inc.
gang scrambled toward the Super Heroes.
Unfortunately, they didn't make it in time. The
griffin bit down on the line, snapping it as if it
were a thread. The crime fighters flew backward,
toward the approaching group.

BAM!

They slammed into the gang, taking
everyone down like bowling pins. By the time
they all got to their feet, the creature was gone.

CHAPTER 2

THE MISSING MONSTER

"Thanks for the save, Batwoman and Batman," Daphne said. "For a minute there, I thought we were goners."

"You're welcome," Batwoman replied. "It's just too bad that the griffin got away."

Shaggy and Scooby-Doo turned to leave. "Well, now that the Super Heroes are here," Shaggy said, "we can all just head back to the Mystery Machine and . . ."

"Not so fast, guys," Fred interrupted as he grabbed Shaggy's collar and Scooby's tail. "It looks like we have a real mystery on our hands."

Shaggy shook his head. "Like, I really hate when he says that."

"Reah," Scooby agreed.

"It's a mystery because griffins aren't real," Velma explained.

"True," Batman agreed. "Someone or something is behind the creature we saw."

"And what happened to Dr. Coats?" Daphne asked. She told the crime fighters how the archaeologist disappeared just after opening the cursed crypt.

"I don't believe in curses," Batman said. He turned to Batwoman. "But we should split up and look for both Dr. Coats *and* the missing monster."

Batwoman nodded. "I agree."

"Our team can split up and help too," Fred suggested.

Batman's lips tightened. "Fine," he muttered. "But if you see the monster, stand back and let us handle it."

Shaggy raised both hands. "Like, no argument here, Mister Batman, sir!"

Velma, Shaggy, and Scooby-Doo followed Batwoman into one part of the museum. Fred and Daphne went with Batman in the opposite direction. The Dark Knight led the way past many of the museum's exhibits, but there was no sign of the griffin anywhere. All was quiet and still.

"How can such a big monster get away so easily?" Daphne asked.

"I don't know," Fred replied. "But maybe the right clue will give us the answer."

The group made their way down another large corridor. It was lined with statues of all shapes and sizes. The biggest one was a statue of a Cyclops. The one-eyed creature held a large club in one hand. Batman moved past the Cyclops, still scanning the area.

Daphne stopped and gazed up at the towering Cyclops. A chill ran down her spine when the creature's one eye . . . blinked.

"F-F-F-Fred," was all she could get out as she pointed up at the statue.

Fred stopped in his tracks as the Cyclops transformed from a statue into a real monster. It turned toward the Dark Knight.

With lightning speed, the creature raised its club and brought it down toward Batman.

"Look out!" Fred shouted.

The crime fighter leaped to the side just as the Cyclops struck.

BAM!

Its weapon smashed onto the floor where Batman had just been standing. The creature snarled and charged toward the hero, swinging its club back and forth.

WHHP! WHHP! WHHP!

Batman flipped backward, narrowly escaping the powerful blows. Then, just as the beast raised its club high above its head, the Dark Knight went on the attack. He landed a flying kick against the monster's chest, making it stumble backward. Batman didn't let up. He followed with several punches. His cape fluttered behind him as he finished with a spinning kick.

WHAP!

The Cyclops flew backward, slamming into a marble statue. Fred and Daphne rushed over and pushed against the statue to keep it from toppling over.

ROOOOOOOAR!

The beast roared with anger as it scrambled to its feet. It charged at Batman, but the hero was ready for it. The Dark Knight pulled a set of bolas from his Utility Belt. He twirled the heavy balls on the end of long ropes over his head before letting them fly. The weapon wrapped tightly around the Cyclops's legs.

WHAM!

The giant smashed face-first onto the floor. Batman ran toward the downed monster but didn't get there in time. The Cyclops snapped the ropes and sprang to its feet. It swung its club at the Caped Crusader who somersaulted over the blow. The monster didn't continue the attack. Instead, it sprinted into a nearby chamber.

WHHP! Batman flung something at the beast as it ran.

Fred and Daphne darted up to the Dark Knight.

"First a griffin, and now a Cyclops," Fred said. "Talk about a mythical mystery."

"And it's getting away," Daphne added.

"This monster isn't getting away so easily," Batman said. "I put a tracking device on its back. Maybe it will lead us to whoever is behind all this."

The three ran out of the hall and into the nearby chamber. The large room was full of more exhibits and ancient treasures. It didn't have any other exits. It also didn't have a mythical Cyclops.

"It's gone," Fred said, glancing around.

Batman's jaw tightened as he scanned the area. Then he reached down and picked up a bat-shaped device with a blinking red light—his tracker.

The three looked all over the large room, but there was no place for such a large creature to hide.

"Where could it go?" Fred asked. He checked around all the display cases for secret hatches or doorways. "There's no other way out of here."

Daphne rubbed her chin as she examined a nearby air vent. "The only way out of here is this vent," she said. "And the Cyclops was way too big to fit through it."

Batman squinted up at the vent. "There's more to this mystery than meets the eye."

CHAPTER 3

MORE MISSING MONSTERS

Velma, Shaggy, and Scooby-Doo trailed after Batwoman as they made their way through another part of the museum.

"Like, I don't know about you, Scoob," Shaggy said, "but visiting a museum sure is a lot more fun when you're not on the lookout for a scary monster."

"Roo said it," Scooby-Doo agreed as he nervously glanced around.

Batwoman stopped and put a hand next to her ear. "Make that monsters," she said. "Batman just said they had a run-in with a Cyclops."

"You mean the big, scary guy with only one eye?" Shaggy asked.

"Hmm . . . another creature from Greek mythology," Velma added. "And another one of the monsters that's carved on the crypt. I think that may be a clue."

"It could be," Batwoman agreed as she scanned the area. "It got away from Batman and the others, so keep an eye out."

"Keep an *eye* out?" Shaggy giggled nervously. "Like, that'd be funny if I wasn't so terrified."

The group continued on until they reached a long chamber full of medieval exhibits. Suits of armor lined both walls of the room while glass cases protected long broadswords and crossbows.

Velma beamed. "This is one of my favorite parts of the museum," she said. "Knights in shining armor. Kings and queens in castles."

"Like, how can you get so excited at a time like this?" Shaggy asked.

"Unlike you, I *can* enjoy a museum and look for scary monsters at the same time," Velma replied. "It's a gift."

Scooby-Doo aimed a shaking paw at the other end of the room. "How about now?"

Everyone froze as a terrifying creature entered the opposite side of the hall. The towering beast had a man's body with a bull's head. It pawed at the floor with one of its hooves as it aimed its long, sharp horns at the group.

Velma adjusted her glasses for a better look. "The minotaur! That's the half man, half bull that guarded a special maze."

The creature snorted as it stepped forward.

"Like, I think I met your brother once on a haunted farm near here," Shaggy said to the beast.

The minotaur didn't reply. Instead, it lowered its head and charged toward them.

CLOMP! CLOMP! CLOMP! CLOMP!

"Stay back," Batwoman told the others as she ran toward the creature.

Shaggy and Scooby-Doo hugged each other in fright. "Like, I don't think Batwoman is going to win in a head-butting contest."

Before Batwoman and the minotaur collided, the Super Hero dropped to the floor. She slid across the smooth tiles like a baseball player sliding into home plate. As she passed between the monster's legs, she pulled out her grapnel. Once she was behind the angry beast, she turned and fired.

POP-WRRR!

The hook wrapped around the creature's waist, but the beast kept charging forward. Shaggy, Scooby, and Velma dove for cover. Unfortunately, Velma's glasses flew off her head as she tumbled.

"My glasses," Velma said as she crawled across the floor. She patted the tiles in front of her. "I can't see a thing without my glasses!"

Before the minotaur could get any farther, Batwoman sprang to her feet and jerked the line. The monster grasped at the air above Velma's head before being flung backward. It slammed against the floor, sliding back toward Batwoman.

The crime fighter leaped into the air, her cape flowing behind her. She brought both boots down on the monster just as it got to its feet.

BAM! The beast flew back, skidding past Velma as she crawled along in her search.

The minotaur stumbled to its feet and unwrapped the line from around its waist. Then it grabbed the line with one hand and jerked Batwoman off her feet. The beast swung the crime fighter around, finally flinging her out of the hall.

The monster glanced down and spotted Velma on the floor. It snorted as it moved closer, reaching out for its unsuspecting victim.

Tk-tk-tk-tk-tk-tk-tk-tk!

A rattle came from the nearby suits of armor. The minotaur whipped its head around and examined the rows of metal suits. The beast lowered its head and charged.

KRASH! It smashed two of the empty suits, and metal pieces flew everywhere.

Farther down the line, Shaggy and Scooby hid inside two suits of armor. They shivered with fear, making their armor rattle.

"Like, quit shaking, Scoob," Shaggy whispered. "You're going to give us away."

"I can't help it, Raggy," Scooby said with a whimper.

"Yeah," Shaggy agreed. "Like, I can't help it either, pal."

KRASH! The minotaur swung its long horns and knocked over two more suits of armor. They were empty too.

The beast squinted as it moved down the line. It finally spotted the source of the rattling. Two suits of armor quivered, and one had a long, brown tail poking out from behind. The minotaur snorted and pawed the floor, ready to charge.

POOF!

A small pellet hit the floor at the monster's feet. A cloud of smoke burst from the pellet and surrounded the beast in a hazy cloud.

BAM! Batwoman landed a flying kick, and the minotaur flew out of the cloud and skidded across the floor.

Meanwhile, Velma's hand finally fell onto her glasses. She put them on just in time to see the monster scramble to its hooves. Batwoman gave chase as the beast made a break for it.

Velma ran up to the suits of armor. "Quit fooling around, guys," she said. "The monster's getting away!"

Shaggy and Scooby-Doo hopped after Velma as she followed Batwoman. The two friends left a trail of armor along the way.

The group ran after the monster as it dashed out of the room. It darted into a corridor to the right, disappearing from sight. When Batwoman, Velma, Shaggy, and Scooby turned the corner, the hallway was empty. Suddenly, Batman, Fred, and Daphne appeared at the other end.

"Did you see where it went?" Batwoman asked.

"Where what went?" Batman asked.

"Like, a big scary minotaur," Shaggy answered. "Long, sharp horns and a real bad attitude?"

"We didn't see anything like that," Fred explained. "And nothing ran past us."

Batwoman scanned the area. "Where could it have gone? There's no other way out of here."

Daphne examined the nearby wall. "Just more of these air vents."

CHAPTER 4

SEEING DOUBLE

"Like, how could a big, scary monster fit through an air vent?" Shaggy asked.

"Well, it was certainly impossible for it to get past us without anyone seeing it," Fred added.

Velma raised a finger. "Sherlock Holmes often said this about solving mysteries," she explained. "If you get rid of the impossible, whatever is left, no matter how unlikely it may be, has to be true."

"Good advice," Batman agreed as he scanned the nearby air vent. "And I may know who's behind this," he explained. "But to be sure, we need to find a room in this museum without any air vents."

"And another monster," Batwoman added, glancing around.

"Maybe we should stick together this time," Daphne suggested.

"Good idea," Batman agreed as he led the way down the hallway.

"Good idea?" Shaggy asked. "Like, that's the best idea I've heard all day."

"Reah!" Scooby agreed, nodding his head. "The best!"

The group cautiously made their way through the museum. Batman and Batwoman were in the lead as everyone kept an eye out for more monsters.

As they entered another large hall, Batman held up a hand. Everyone froze and didn't say a word.

Bam-bam-bam-bam!

There was a pounding noise ahead. Both crime fighters pulled Batarangs from their Utility Belts and inched forward. The noise grew louder as they approached a supply closet. The Super Heroes moved to each side of the door and raised their weapons. Batman reached out and threw open the door.

"Dr. Coats?" Velma asked.

The archaeologist panted as she stumbled out of the closet. "Thank goodness you got me out of there." She jumped when she spotted the crime fighters. "What are you doing here?"

"Like, only fighting all the monsters that your creepy, cursed crypt created," Shaggy replied.

"Monsters?" asked Dr. Coats. "What monsters? What are you talking about?"

Velma went on to describe all the mythical creatures that had appeared after Dr. Coats had opened the crypt and disappeared.

"But I didn't open the crypt," Dr. Coats explained. "Someone grabbed me and locked me in this closet this morning. I've been here all day."

"Did you see who grabbed you?" Batwoman asked.

The archaeologist shook her head. "No, it all happened so fast."

Daphne put her hands on her hips. "Well then who opened the crypt?"

Batman's lips tightened. "Hmm . . . it's another clue."

GRRRRRR . . .

"Gee, Scoob," Shaggy said. "I'm hungry too, but tell your stomach to keep it down, will ya?"

Scooby-Doo shook his head. "Rat wasn't my stomach, Raggy."

Shaggy grabbed his own belly. "Well, it wasn't mine. And if it wasn't yours . . ." Both he and Scooby slowly turned their heads to see *three* heads staring at them. Each one snarled, baring rows of sharp teeth. It was none other than Cerberus!

GRRRRRRRRRRR . . .

"Zoinks!" Shaggy shouted as he leaped into Scooby-Doo's arms. "It's the three-headed dog monster!"

Dr. Coats and the Mystery Inc. gang scattered as the crime fighters went on the attack. They both threw their Batarangs at the giant dog. Two of the beast's heads easily caught the weapons in their mouths.

KRAK-KRAK!

They bit down, snapping the Batarangs in two.

The beast sprang forward, landing between Batman and Batwoman. They each dodged vicious bites from one of the snapping dog heads.

"Is this one of the monsters you were talking about?" Dr. Coats asked Fred as he helped her to her feet.

"It is," Fred replied. "And Batman has a plan. Is there a part of the museum that doesn't have air vents?"

"What?" the archaeologist asked.

KRASH!

Cerberus crashed into a wall after he charged Batman. The Dark Knight just barely flipped out of the way in time.

"Air-conditioning vents," Daphne explained. "Does every room in the museum have them?"

POP!

Batwoman fired a net over two of the dog's heads. Unfortunately, the third head ripped the net away with its sharp teeth.

"The Egyptian wing," Dr. Coats replied. She pointed past the battle to the large room next door. "There aren't any vents in there because we need to keep the mummies at the right temperature."

Fred cupped his hands around his mouth. "Batman!"

The Dark Knight quickly ducked under a set of snapping jaws. "I heard," he replied. "Get ready to move."

Batman and Batwoman backed away as the Caped Crusader flung three explosive Batarangs at the creature.

POW-POW-POW!

The beast stumbled from the blasts. As smoke filled the room, the monster dog loped into the Egyptian wing.

Batman and Batwoman sprinted after it, with Fred, Daphne, Velma, and Dr. Coats close behind.

The group entered the large room full of many different artifacts from ancient Egypt. Just as Dr. Coats had said, it didn't have any air vents. It also didn't have a monster.

"Where did it go?" asked Velma.

"Wait a minute," said Daphne. "Look!" She pointed at a large clay pot as it swayed back and forth on its stand.

WOBBLE-WOBBLE-WOBBLE!

The crime fighters moved forward, preparing for another attack.

Instead of a mythical creature, Shaggy climbed out of the pot. He laughed nervously. "I guess you found my hiding spot." He dusted off his pants and shirt.

"You didn't see where the monster went, did you?" Fred asked.

Shaggy shrugged. "Nope. Sorry."

Just then, Scooby-Doo ambled into the room. He walked up to Shaggy and sniffed his pants.

"You smell funny, Raggy," he said.

Shaggy laughed nervously. "You'd smell funny too if you had used a dirty old pot for a hiding spot."

"Hiding spot?" asked a familiar voice. "Like, I found a great one!" A second Shaggy jutted a thumb over his shoulder as he walked into the room. He froze when he saw the other version of himself. "Like, what's going on here?"

"Two Shaggys?" Daphne asked.

The second Shaggy marched up to the first one. "Like, what's the big idea stealing my face, fella?"

The first Shaggy shook his head. "No way, pal. You stole *my* face!"

"How can we tell them apart?" Fred asked.

Velma crossed her arms. "I wonder if we should discuss this over dinner."

The first Shaggy threw up his arms. "How can anyone eat at a time like this?!" he asked.

The second Shaggy held up a finger. "Now wait just a minute," he said. "Like, let's hear her out."

"Not hungry?" Daphne asked as she rolled her eyes. "I know who the imposter is now."

"Yeah." Fred nodded. "He's also the one who doesn't say *like* in every other sentence."

Batman and Batwoman moved in.

The first Shaggy backed away from the group. "I guess I didn't do enough character research," he said as a wide grin stretched across his face.

The fake Shaggy's eyes flashed yellow before his face began to droop and shift. His entire body turned dark brown and grew three times its size. Finally, a towering figure looked down at them with a toothy grin and glowing eyes.

"I knew it," Batman said.

CHAPTER 5

THE GRAND CLOSING

"Oh, my! It's Gotham City super-criminal Clayface!" Velma announced. "He was formerly known as the famous actor Matt Hagen. But too much face-shaping cream turned him into a monster with only one thing on his muddy mind—revenge!"

"I'll bet he's the one who opened the crypt in the first place," Fred added. "Disguised as Dr. Coats."

"Think you have it all figured out, don't you?" Clayface asked with a snarl. "But you may not know that I'm after whatever priceless treasures are inside that crypt." His giant fists formed into spiked balls. "And I'm not about to let a couple of bats and a bunch of meddling kids stop me!" He swung his weapons down.

BAM!

Batman and Batwoman dove for cover as the criminal smashed the floor with his spiked fists.

Batwoman glanced over her shoulder. "Get to safety!" she ordered as she pulled two Batarangs from her Utility Belt. Batman did the same.

The rest of the group scattered as Batman and Batwoman attacked the huge criminal.

WHP-WHP! WHP-WHP! Batman and Batwoman flung the weapons at Clayface. All four Batarangs hit their target, but they had no effect. They disappeared into the villain's body.

"Cute toys," Clayface said with a chuckle. "Want them back?" The fiend blasted the four Batarangs from one of his spiked fists.

FWOP-FWOP-FWOP-FWOP!

The crime fighters shielded themselves with their capes as their own weapons flew back at them.

"We have to help them somehow," Daphne said.

"But how?" asked Dr. Coats. "That Clayface person seems unstoppable."

"Don't worry," Fred said. "I have a plan."

"Oh, boy, Scoob," Shaggy said. "Like, what do you say we find a nice, quiet place to sit this one out? The snack bar, maybe?"

"Oh, no you don't," Fred warned. "I need everyone's help." A grin stretched across his face. "It's trappin' time!"

After Fred gave everyone instructions, they split up and headed for different parts of the museum. Meanwhile, Batman and Batwoman continued to battle Clayface. The villain turned one of his hands into a long spike and jabbed it at Batman. The Caped Crusader somersaulted over the attack with ease.

Clayface's other hand melted into a long, vine-like tendril. It struck at Batwoman like a giant snake and then wrapped around her body. She was just quick enough to pull out a Batarang and chop through the tendril before it squeezed her too tightly. The crime fighter backflipped to safety as the severed tendril snaked back to Clayface and reattached itself.

The crime fighters battled the enraged villain until they were back at the front of the museum near the open Greek crypt. To Batman and Batwoman's surprise, they suddenly had plenty of backup.

Daphne darted in with a mace in both hands, the metal club held at the ready. Fred held the short handle of a flail as he twirled the spiked ball that dangled from the weapon's chain. Velma crept closer behind a large Roman shield, while Dr. Coats held a large dinosaur bone like a baseball bat. Along with Batman and Batwoman, they surrounded Clayface.

"Well, look at what we have here," the villain said with a chuckle. He raised his hands high above his head. "Looks like you got me." He gave a devious grin. "Or . . . we can keep the Greek theme going. What do you say?"

Clayface grew taller and wider as his body changed into the scariest mythical creature yet. His lower body formed into a scaly beast with four legs and a long tail. Meanwhile, his upper body stretched into nine long necks with a dragon's head at the end of each. All the heads hissed and bared rows of razor-sharp teeth.

"Oh, boy," Velma said. "Not the hydra."

"That's right," said the nine heads in unison. "A little something for everybody!"

SNAP-SNAP! SNAP-SNAP-SNAP-SNAP!

Everyone braced themselves as all the hydra's heads attacked at once. Velma blocked the biting jaws with her shield, while Dr. Coats and Fred batted them away. The head attacking Daphne bit down on her mace and lifted her off the ground.

"Freeze tech," Batman ordered. "Now!"

The Dark Knight removed several blue Batarangs from his Utility Belt.

WHP! He launched one at the head holding Daphne's mace. When the weapon struck the beast, ice crackled over the head until it broke off from the neck.

KRASH!

The head shattered into a million pieces when it hit the floor.

Batwoman followed Batman's lead.

WHP-WHP! She hurtled two of the special weapons toward the heads attacking Fred and Dr. Coats. The Batarangs froze those heads too.

"No fair, Bats," said the remaining hydra heads. "Using Mr. Freeze's tech against me!"

"You think scaring innocent citizens is fair?" Batwoman asked.

"I'll show you fair," the monster replied. "You remember the story of the hydra, don't you, Doc?"

The archaeologist's eyes widened. "Oh, no."

The Clayface hydra laughed. "Oh, yes."

For every head that was missing, two more formed in its place. Now they were up against a dragon with *twelve* heads!

As Fred fought off two hydra heads, he glanced over at the crypt. Shaggy and Scooby were in position. "Now, Shaggy!" he shouted.

Shaggy shivered as he opened the crypt door a little wider. He glanced nervously at Scooby and cleared his throat.

"Like, hurry, Scoob," Shaggy said, loud enough for the monster to hear. "Let's get this treasure out of here and hide it somewhere else."

"Reah!" Scooby-Doo agreed, speaking just as loudly. "We don't want Rayface to find the riceless treasure."

All twelve of the hydra heads spun to glare at Shaggy and Scooby. The two friends gulped as the dragon left the battle and galloped toward them. As the monster ran, it slowly shrunk until Clayface ran in his original form.

"You're not hiding nothin'!" Clayface shouted as he rounded on the two friends.

"That crypt is airtight, Batman," Fred said.

A smile pulled at the Dark Knight's lips. With lightning speed, he flung a blue Batarang toward the criminal's back.

WHP-KRACLE!

Ice spread across Clayface's back, causing him to stumble. He tripped and fell straight into the crypt.

"Come on, Scoob!" Shaggy shouted as he and Scooby rushed forward.

BAM!

The two friends slammed the door shut.

POP!

Batwoman fired her grapnel. In a flash, the hook and line wrapped around the stone structure, keeping it shut tight. Everyone hurried forward as Clayface pounded on the inside of the crypt.

"We figured if Clayface could escape through the air vents, then we needed to find an airtight way to hold him," Daphne explained.

"And the crypt seemed to be the best thing around," Velma added.

"Good job, everyone" Batman said.

"But what about the treasures inside?" Dr. Coats asked.

"You'll get them and the crypt back once we transfer the entire thing to Arkham Asylum," Batwoman replied. "Until then, Clayface will spend time with what's inside, just like he wanted."

Scooby-Doo giggled. "Rooby-dooby-doo!"

CLAYFACE

Real Name: Matt Hagen

Occupation: Professional Criminal

Base: Gotham City

Height: Varies

Weight: Varies

Eyes: Varies

Hair: Varies

Powers/Abilities:
Shape-shifting and superhuman strength. He is also a professional actor and skilled impressionist.

Biography: Formerly a big name in the movie industry, actor Matt Hagen had his face, and career, ruined in a tragic car crash. Hoping to regain his good looks, Hagan accepted the help of ruthless businessman Roland Daggett, who gave him a special cream that allowed Hagen to reshape his face like clay. Hopelessly addicted, Hagen was caught stealing more cream, and Daggett forced him to consume an entire barrel as punishment. However, instead of killing Hagen, the large dose turned him into a muddy monster with revenge on his mind.

- As Clayface, Matt Hagen is no longer human. His entire body is made of muddy clay, which grants him incredible shape-shifting abilities as well as super-strength.

- Clayface's power is limited only by his imagination. He can turn his limbs into lethal weapons by willing his muddy body into whatever shape he desires.

- Drawing upon his shape-shifting abilities and his experience as an actor, Clayface assumes the shapes and voices of others. These abilities make him a very difficult foe to detect.

BIOGRAPHIES

photo by M. A. Steele

Michael Anthony Steele has been in the entertainment industry for more than 28 years, writing for television, movies, and video games. He has authored more than 120 books for exciting characters and brands including Batman, Superman, Wonder Woman, Spider-Man, Shrek, Scooby-Doo, WISHBONE, LEGO City, Garfield, Night at the Museum, and The Penguins of Madagascar. Steele lives on a ranch in Texas, but he enjoys meeting his readers when he visits schools and libraries all across the country. For more information, visit MichaelAnthonySteele.com.

photo by Dario Brizuela

Dario Brizuela works traditionally and digitally in many different illustration styles. His work can be found in a wide range of properties, including Star Wars Tales, DC Super Hero Girls, DC Super Friends, Transformers, Scooby-Doo! Team-Up, and more. Brizuela lives in Buenos Aires, Argentina.

GLOSSARY

archaeologist (ar-kee-AH-luh-jist)—a scientist who studies how people lived in the past

attitude (AT-i-tood)—your opinions or feelings about someone or something

chamber (CHAYM-buhr)—a large room

corridor (KOR-uh-dur)—a long hallway or passage in a building

crypt (KRIPT)—a chamber used as a grave

curse (KURS)—an evil spell meant to harm someone

exhibit (eg-ZIB-it)—a display that usually includes objects and information to show and tell people about a certain subject

grapnel (GRAP-nuhl)—a grappling hook connected to a rope that can be fired like a gun

hijab (HEE-jahb)—a traditional covering for the hair and neck that is worn by Muslim women

mythology (mi-THOL-uh-jee)—old or ancient stories told again and again that help connect people with their past

sponsor (SPON-sur)—a person or company that pays for an event to take place

tendril (TEN-drel)—a long, slender limb or vine

THINK ABOUT IT

1. Batman and the Mystery Inc. gang team up with Batwoman in this story. Do you think they could have foiled Clayface's plot without her help? Explain your answer.

2. Clayface's plan is to steal whatever treasure is hidden inside the ancient Greek crypt. The story never reveals what that treasure might be. What kind of valuable items do you think are hidden inside it?

3. Batman and Batwoman have Batarangs that use freeze tech created by Mr. Freeze. Why would heroes want to use technology created by a Super-Villain?

WRITE ABOUT IT

1. Which hero in this story is your favorite? Write a paragraph explaining who you like the best and why.

2. Clayface has the power to transform into any type of mythical monster. If you had his power, what monster of myth would you become? Write a short paragraph describing your monster and then draw a picture of it.

3. At the end of the story, Clayface gets trapped inside the Greek crypt. What happens next? Write a new chapter describing how Batman and Batwoman transfer him to Arkham Asylum or how he escapes. You decide!

READ THEM ALL!